The Dead Sea Squirrels Series

THE
DEAD SEA
SQUiRRELS

Risky River Rescue

Mike Nawrocki

Illustrated by Luke Séguin-Magee

Tyndale House Publishers
Carol Stream, Illinois

Visit Tyndale's website for kids at tyndale.com/kids.

Visit the author's website at mikenawrocki.com.

Tyndale is a registered trademark of Tyndale House Ministries. The Tyndale Kids logo is a trademark of Tyndale House Ministries.

The Dead Sea Squirrels is a registered trademark of Michael L. Nawrocki.

Risky River Rescue

Designed by Libby Dykstra

Edited by Deborah King

Published in association with the literary agency of Brentwood Studios, 1550 McEwen, Suite 300 PNB 17, Franklin, TN 37067.

For manufacturing information regarding this product, please call 1-855-277-9400.

For information about special discounts for bulk purchases, please contact Tyndale House Publishers at csresponse@tyndale.com, or call 1-855-277-9400.

Library of Congress Cataloging-in-Publication Data

A catalog record for this book is available from the Library of Congress.

ISBN 978-1-4964-4985-6

Printed in the United States of America

28 27 26 25 24 23 22
7   6   5   4   3   2   1

To my father- and mother-in-law, Karl and Lucia Klepp-Gomez, whose love and legacy live on in the lives of their grandchildren.

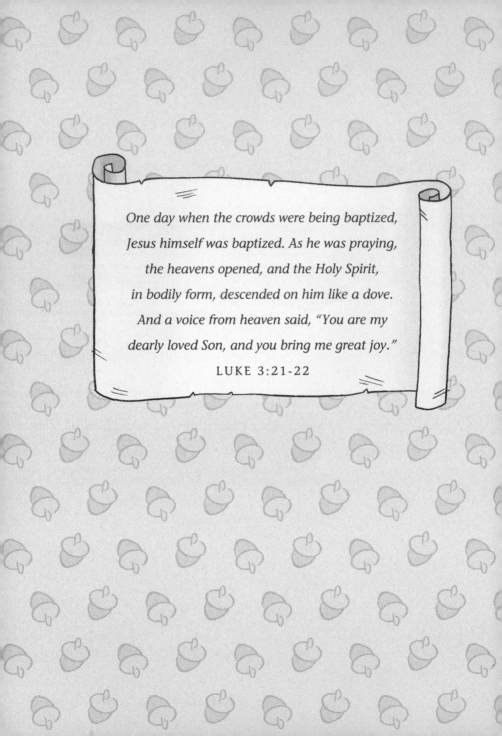

One day when the crowds were being baptized,
Jesus himself was baptized. As he was praying,
the heavens opened, and the Holy Spirit,
in bodily form, descended on him like a dove.
And a voice from heaven said, "You are my
dearly loved Son, and you bring me great joy."

LUKE 3:21-22

BUT WAIT!

BEFORE WE START...

Who are the Dead Sea Squirrels?

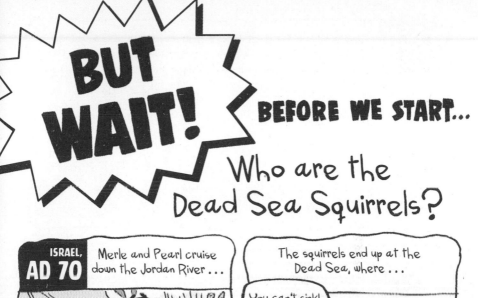

ISRAEL, AD 70

Merle and Pearl cruise down the Jordan River...

...on the vacation of a lifetime!

The squirrels end up at the Dead Sea, where...

You can't sink! I've always wanted to not sink!

Couldn't you have just worn your floaties in the lake back home?

Soon the two salty squirrels are hot, thirsty, and desperate for shade. Then they spot a cave.

Merle's sense of adventure lures him into the cave, despite Pearl's protests.

If God wanted you to go into a cave, he would have made you a bat.

Ten-year-old Michael Gomez is spending the summer at the Dead Sea with his professor dad and his best friend, Justin.

While exploring a cave (without his dad's permission), Michael discovers two dried-out, salt-covered critters and stashes them in his backpack.

Michael sneaks the squirrels back home with him to Tennessee.

He sets them up like posable action figures on his dresser—under an open window.

While Michael is sleeping, a thunderstorm rolls in, and it begins to rain . . .

. . . rehydrating the squirrels!

Up and kicking again after almost 2,000 years, Merle and Pearl Squirrel have great stories and advice to share with the modern world.

They are the Dead Sea Squirrels!

But the Dead Sea Squirrels' adventures don't end there. Merle and Pearl soon find out that things are

a whole lot different

from the first century!

For one thing, there are self-filling fresh water bowls . . .

an endless supply of walnuts and chicken nuggets . . .

Thank you, chickens, for your nuggets!

and much fancier places to live!

I could get used to this!

Plus, they get to go to fifth grade (as long as no one sees them)!

Stay still, Merle! Pretend you are stuffed!

But even in quiet Walnut Creek, Tennessee, danger is never too far away!

Nice kitty...

What if Mom and Dad find out?!

And a man in a suit and sunglasses who wants nothing more than to get his hands on the squirrels ... does!

HELP!!!

Now it's back to the Holy Land to rescue the squirrels!

MICHAEL!

CHAPTER 1

"Couldn't you find something roomier!?" Merle shouted from inside a backpack resting on a spare tire in the trunk of Ruben's car. "And by the way, it's pitch-black in here! I'm not a fan of the dark!" Having gotten himself trapped in a cave for 2,000 years, Merle's uneasiness was certainly understandable. "Can I ask what's wrong with the back seat?!"

"Nothing is wrong with the back seat. It's a perfectly good back seat," Ruben called back over the road and engine noise from his spot in the driver's seat as they jetted down a highway in Israel.

"Whatcha got in here?" Merle said as he shifted uncomfortably. Sharing the pack with him were a number of Ruben's supplies, including a change of clothes, a bag of trail mix, a tin of tea leaves, and a bottle of honey. Ruben never went anywhere without his tea supplies. "I'd love a bit more elbow room."

"You don't have elbows!" Ruben hollered.

"You, sir, are ignorant of squirrel anatomy!" Merle replied, rubbing his elbows.

"Whatever!" Ruben barked. "I'm not taking any chances!" This too was understandable on Ruben's part, since the last time he left Merle and Pearl in the back seat of a car in a zipped-up bag, the two resourceful rodents managed to escape. Ruben would have preferred to keep Merle locked up in the giant birdcage that had held him captive for the past several months, but the squirrels had also figured out a way to escape from that. (It was actually their new friend Adriana the alpaca who had picked the lock using a large splinter and her muscular lips, but Ruben

didn't know that.) He had managed
to recapture Merle, but Pearl was now
safely back with the Gomezes.

"Can you at least tell me where we
are going?" Merle pleaded.

"No more questions! You'll find out
when we get there," Ruben replied
sternly. He knew that Pearl and
Michael would be looking for Merle,
and he wasn't going to give away
any information that might aid in
his rescue.

"Are we there yet?" Merle called out.

"I said no more questions!" Ruben
barked.

CHAPTER 2

Have you ever been on a vacation with your family and stayed in a hotel room with two queen-size beds? It's easy and fun if it's just you, your parents, and your sibling. However, if it's you, your parents, your sibling, your two best friends, a squirrel, a donkey, and an alpaca, things can get a little more complicated and a whole lot more stinky.

"What's that smell?" Michael asked groggily from the sofa in their Bethlehem hotel room as the bright morning sunlight peeked around the edges of the curtains. Before anyone could answer his question, the hotel

room door burst open, and Dr. and
Mrs. Gomez entered.

"Up and at 'em!" Michael's dad
exclaimed as he switched on the lights.
"We've got a Merle to rescue!"

"Bagels and Febreze!" Mrs. Gomez
chirped, holding up two shopping
bags, one packed with breakfast
and the other with canisters of
air freshener.

"It smells like a barn in here," Sadie groaned, sitting up in the bed she shared with Jane.

"Sorry," Dusty the donkey replied as he poked his head up from his spot on the floor between the beds.

"Hmm . . ." Adriana the alpaca hummed from inside her bathtub-bed in the bathroom.

"Do those come with cream cheese?" Justin asked, sitting up in his pile of blankets on the floor next to the couch.

"Of course!" Mrs. Gomez replied as she set breakfast up on the TV console. Dr. Gomez drew open the curtains, revealing Pearl, who was just arriving back through the open window from a breakfast run of her own.

"I forgot how much I missed olives!" Pearl said, licking her paws. Unlike in Tennessee, olive trees are plentiful in Israel, and though raw olives can be bitter, Pearl had acquired a taste for them as a young pup in Galilee. This had been her first chance to scavenge for food on her own since being squirrelnapped by Ruben.

While the kids ate their bagels and Mrs. Gomez doused the room with

Febreze, Dr. Gomez retrieved a luggage cart and smuggled Dusty and Adriana out of the hotel the same way they had been snuck in—by pretending they were giant stuffed animals. Pearl also went along for the ride, perched in a frozen pose on Adriana's back. Once past the shocked onlookers in the lobby, Dr. Gomez wheeled the animals across the parking lot.

"I got something for you," he whispered to Dusty and Adriana. Hitched to the back of the van Father Phillip had lent them was a donkey cart filled with hay. "But instead of pulling it, you get to ride in it!"

Before long, the church van, packed with six humans and a squirrel and pulling a cart carrying a donkey and an alpaca munching on hay, rolled out of the Bethlehem hotel parking lot.

CHAPTER 3

CLICK! Merle, his eyes adjusted to total darkness, squinted as tiny pinpricks of light poked through the zipper teeth of his backpack prison.

"Go ahead, you can ask again," Ruben quipped as the trunk popped open on his car.

"Are we there yet?" Merle inquired groggily.

"As a matter of fact we are!" Ruben said smugly, removing the backpack and slamming the trunk shut. He unzipped the backpack just enough for a squirrel head. "Take a look for yourself!"

Merle poked his noggin out and

squinted even more in the bright morning sunlight. They were walking toward a sandy shore dotted with spiky palms and colorful beach umbrellas. A few early-morning swimmers bobbed in the salty blue waters, their faces daubed with thick mud.

Merle knew where they were immediately. Though it had been 2,000 years since he had been on its shores, other than the tourists and beach umbrellas, the Dead Sea had changed very little.

"Why'd you bring me back here?!"
Merle gasped in horror. He had found
out the hard way that the Dead Sea,
with its hot, dry air; overly salty waters;
and deep, dark caves, is completely
inhospitable to tree squirrels. It was the
last place in the world he wanted to be.

"I'm just following orders," Ruben
replied.

Merle's whiskers quivered. "Wait. It's

kind of chilly," he noted. "Why isn't it hot?" The last time he and Pearl were there, it was over 100 degrees. It felt more like 60 now.

"It's winter and it's 8 a.m.," Ruben scoffed.

"Too bad Pearl and I didn't come in the winter last time," Merle said. Maybe their story would have turned out differently if they had. They passed a bather slathered in Dead Sea mud. "Ooh! That looks fun!"

"No time," Ruben said, toting him across the beach toward a dusty old shack. "We have an appointment to keep."

CHAPTER 4

"Do you think Dr. Simon will be here?" Michael asked his dad as their donkey cart–towing van pulled up to the Antiquities Museum in Jerusalem.

"Not likely," Dr. Gomez responded. "But even if he is, I doubt he would show his face." Having recently discovered Dr. Simon's master plan for the world's only talking-animal petting zoo and knowing it was the reason for Merle and Pearl's squirrel-napping, Michael and his dad knew the best bet in finding Merle would be to find Dr. Simon. Dr. Gomez, Michael, Justin, Sadie, and Pearl headed into the museum while Mrs. Gomez and

Jane waited outside with Dusty and Adriana.

"I'm sorry. Dr. Simon is not available," Dr. Simon's assistant predictably reported.

"Do you know when he will be back?" Michael inquired.

"No, sir, I'm not sure," she replied.

"Well, can you tell us where he is?" Dr. Gomez followed up.

"No, sir, I cannot."

"How long have you worked for him?" Sadie asked.

"Umm . . . I don't see how that is . . ."

"Is this where the Ark of the Covenant is?" Justin interrupted.

As the group distracted the assistant with further random questions, Pearl slinked unnoticed into Dr. Simon's office. Once inside, she discovered the master site blueprints for the petting zoo, similar to the model at the safe house where Merle and Pearl had been held in Ein Karem.

"BabbleLand Animal Park," the title of the top blueprint read. Dr. Simon's handwritten phrases were scribbled in the margins. Pearl pored over the notes as she tried to take them all in:

"The only zoo where cuddly creatures talk to you," read one phrase.

"Small talk with the livestock," read
another.

"Holy Land–themed rides, live
shows, restaurants! BabbleLand—
Scratch, Schmooze, Snack, and Smile!"

"He's obviously still working on his
marketing language," Pearl whispered.

At the bottom of the blueprints, in
small type, Pearl found these words:
"Adjoining the existing Zoological
Gardens and Aquarium in Jerusalem."

"Aha!" Pearl said. She rolled up the
blueprints and dragged them out of
Dr. Simon's office and past his assistant, who was still being barraged
with questions.

"Why do bugs buzz around lights at
night?" Michael asked.

"I have absolutely no idea," the assistant replied, highly annoyed.

"What did they do at night before electricity?" wondered Justin.

CHAPTER 5

"I almost had it!" Dr. Simon cried as he burst through the front door of the Dead Sea beach house. His sudden arrival saved Ruben the trouble of answering any more of Merle's questions about what they were doing there. "I saw him with my own eyes— sunbathing on a rock, singing a song as clear as day!" Dr. Simon collapsed into a faded armchair in the living room before burying his face in his hands and whimpering.

"Almost had what?" Ruben inquired, breaking an awkward silence.

"A Lizard of Judah!" Dr. Simon exploded. "I have long heard rumors

of its existence." He stood to re-
create the moment. "I crept closer
. . . closer . . ." He tiptoed toward
the coffee table and the TV remote.
"I reached out my hand . . . slowly
. . . silently . . ." He bent down as
his hand inched toward the remote.
"And BOOM!" He shot up, startling
Ruben and Merle. "Just like that, he
was gone!" Dr. Simon marched back
to his armchair and sat down with
a thud.

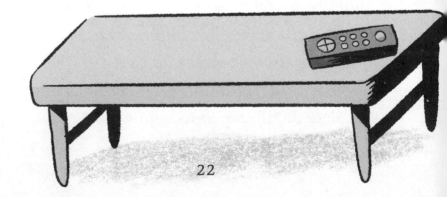

Merle nodded. Squirrels, when in shape, were equally speedy. "What song?" Merle asked.

"What?" Dr. Simon barked.

"What song did the lizard sing?" Merle clarified.

"I don't know, some sort of an 'I'm a happy lizard lying in the sun' song. I had never heard it before."

"I'm a happy lizard, lying in the sun," Merle sang. "I'm a happy lizard . . . I sure am . . . having fun."

"That's not how it went!" the doctor shouted.

"Sir, if I may ask," Ruben ventured, "why a lizard? Who wants to pet a talking lizard? They're so dry and scaly, not soft and fluffy and cuddly like a squirrel."

PETTING ZOO

Dr. Simon was losing patience. "It's my talking-animal petting zoo, and I'll have any kind of animal I want in it!"

"Yes, sir." Ruben cowered.

"And speaking of squirrels, you need to get this one out of the country. With the Gomezes snooping around, we can't take any chances," Dr. Simon said.

Hearing this was a relief to Merle if only because it meant they'd be leaving the Dead Sea.

"Good idea," Ruben answered. "Will we be flying or driving?"

"Neither," Dr. Simon responded, handing Ruben a sheet of paper with a sketch of a map on it—a zigzaggy line along the Jordan River, from the Dead Sea north to the Sea of Galilee. "You'll be rowing and walking."

CHAPTER 6

THIS IS ENORMOUS!

Pearl marveled as the Gomezes' van pulled up to the BabbleLand construction zone, nestled in the hills of southwest Jerusalem.

"It looks nearly finished," Sadie noted. The park was, in fact, nearing completion, and at the moment, a crane was lifting a large section of a roller coaster into place. A large fence lined the perimeter of the park, with a single entrance that appeared to be for construction workers.

"How are we going to get in?" Justin wondered, staring at the fence.

"I've got an idea!" Michael stated slyly.

Sometimes acting like you belong somewhere is much less notice- able than trying not to be noticed. That's why the sight of two adults, one carrying a set of blueprints, and four children walking an alpaca and a donkey on leashes inside a future zoo didn't attract much attention among the workers.

"Excuse me, sir!" Dr. Gomez called confidently to a man directing a group of workers. "We're looking for Dr. Simon."

"Dr. Simon is collecting specimens," the man reported. "I believe along the Dead Sea."

At the mention of the Dead Sea, Pearl gasped from inside Michael's backpack.

"You okay?" the man asked Michael.

"Ahem." Michael cleared his throat. "Did you say the Dead Sea?"

"Yes, near Kalia Beach. Follow me," the man said, then led them through a clump of arched palm trees to the Dead Sea region of the park. "This is where the Lizard of Judah will reside alongside the Dead Sea Squirrels," he reported, pointing out the netted enclosure containing cliffs and caves fashioned from artificial rocks.

"We're not from the Dead Sea," Pearl clarified from the backpack.

"What was that?" the man asked.

"Oh, nothing," Michael responded in his best falsetto voice, trying to imitate Pearl.

"Dr. Simon has got the squirrels. He just needs the lizard."

"Where are the squirrels, currently?" Dr. Gomez asked, testing the waters.

The man shrugged. "Nobody knows but Dr. Simon. The entire zoo collection is being held in a number of secret locations all over the country. But soon, they will all be here!" he said proudly. "Including donkeys!" He stroked Dusty's mane. "However, I wasn't aware of plans for an alpaca."

Adriana replied with a "Hmm . . ."

"We'll have to clear that up with Dr. Simon," Dr. Gomez told the man as they headed back toward the parking lot.

CHAPTER 7

"In honor of your row across the Dead Sea, I'm making you a boat!" Merle goaded Ruben from inside his backpack.

"I'm not in the mood, Merle," Ruben griped as he tossed the backpack into the stern of the rowboat and pushed off from shore.

"It's always a great time for origami!" Merle chirped as he folded the paper map Dr. Simon had given to Ruben into the shape of a boat. Merle had recently taken up origami during his captivity in Ein Karem and couldn't pass up the opportunity when given a fresh sheet of paper, even in a dark and confined space. "Try not to splash around too much," Merle added as he heard the sound of oars hitting the water and the creak of the oarlocks. "I'd hate to get all salty again."

A couple of months earlier, Ruben had hiked a hundred miles along the Nativity Trail shuttling the squirrels on a donkey. He was not at all happy to be acting as a manual rodent transport once again, especially after an hour of rowing, when the still, cool morning air gave way to a windy and warmer afternoon headwind.

"ARRRGH," Ruben gasped, releasing the oars and falling backward into the bow, exhausted. He had managed to row some distance offshore, and the little rowboat bobbed helplessly on the waters of the great salty sea. The

Dead Sea measures around 30 miles long and 9 miles wide. Thankfully for Ruben, he only needed to row a few miles, but even that was proving to be a challenge.

"Tell you what," Merle said in a well-rested voice. "If you let me out of this backpack, I'll help you row. What am I gonna do, escape?" Merle had a point. There was nowhere to go. The rowboat was a temporary prison for both of them. "I'll take one oar, you take the other," Merle offered.

"Oh, all right," Ruben relented, unzipping the backpack. As he did, the wind caught hold of Merle's origami boat and sent it flying. Ruben nearly fell overboard trying to grab it. "That's our map!" he yelled.

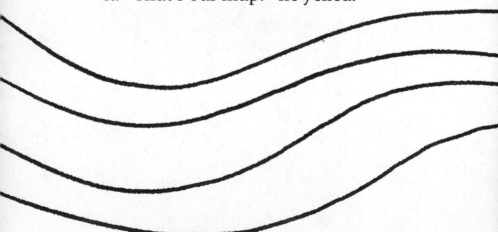

"And a work of art," Merle added
with a smile, despite Ruben's scowl.

"How am I supposed to know where
to go?!" Ruben barked.

"I know from experience that if we
stick to the river, we'll end up at the
Sea of Galilee," Merle replied. "By the
way, we're not rowing up the Jordan,
are we?" Merle had traveled down the
Jordan before and knew that trying
to travel against the current would
be next to impossible.

"We're walking," Ruben replied. "Up the Jordanian side." Jordan is the country that borders Israel to the east and shares the north shore of the Dead Sea with Israel. The Jordan River is the boundary between the two countries.

"Why not just cross the river in Israel?" Merle wondered as they both resumed rowing.

"Because we'll leave a paper trail at an official crossing," Ruben answered. Steering toward the shore, little did he know that this crossing was also leaving a paper trail as the origami boat sailed on the wind back toward Kalia Beach.

CHAPTER 8

Had Highway 1 between Jerusalem
and Jericho been a little narrower,
Michael or Dr. Gomez might have
spotted Dr. Simon driving past them
in the opposite direction. But he was
easy to miss in his faded gray com-
pact sedan among the other motorists
and truckers headed toward Jerusalem
on the divided four-lane freeway.

However, a large church van towing a donkey and an alpaca on an old wooden cart is nearly impossible to miss no matter how wide the road is.

"Ha! You'll never find him!" Dr. Simon snickered to himself as he watched the van receding in his rear-view mirror. He knew that with Merle out of the country, there would be a one-in-a-million chance of the Gomezes finding their missing squirrel.

But even a one-in-a-million chance is still a chance.

Once they arrived at Kalia Beach, the whole group spread out looking for any sign of Merle. Mrs. Gomez, Adriana, and Dusty rushed to check a row of cabanas lining the beach. Out of the corner of his

eye, Dusty spotted a fuzzy brown crea-
ture zip into one of the huts. "Merle!" he
called out. However, when he arrived at
the hut and peeked into it, he was met
with the growl of a tiny shih tzu followed
by the scream of its owner.

PEEPING DONKEY!

the woman
cried out.

Michael, Justin, Sadie, and Pearl ran up and down the beach, tiptoeing over mud-caked sunbathers, searching for any signs of squirrel paw prints. "What's with the mud?" Sadie whispered to Michael.

"I dunno. Minerals or something," Michael replied.

"The high levels of salt and magnesium in the Dead Sea mud are supposed to be good for the skin," Justin added.

"Not to mention a wonderful exfoliant and preservative," Pearl concluded.

They all searched as hard as they could, but with so many people mopping up the mud, any sign of squirrel prints had been erased.

Dr. Gomez and Jane asked around the shops and cafés. "How would I have seen a squirrel?!" a waiter asked. "If you want squirrels, go to Galilee!"

Needless to say, after all the scouring, the search parties came back empty-handed, -pawed, and -hooved.

"They're not here!" Michael lamented as they all regrouped by the van. "What are we gonna do?"

"Yip! Yip!"

Before anyone had a chance to answer, Pearl turned and spotted the shih tzu chasing a small white object blowing toward them across the parking lot. While it would have been understandable for her to disregard it as litter left by beach picnickers, there was something about the shape of the object that caught her eye, something familiar. She scurried to pick it up before the shih tzu could.

"Merle was here!" she squeaked, holding up the origami boat for the others to see. "I'd recognize his work anywhere!"

CHAPTER 9

"It's a map!" Michael exclaimed as he unfolded Merle's origami boat. The hand-drawn chart plotted a path along the eastern shore of the Jordan River toward the Sea of Galilee and Jordan's border with Israel in the north.

"Why Jordan?" Sadie wondered.

"Dr. Simon knows we're close and wants to get us off their trail," Dr. Gomez guessed. "If Ruben snuck out of the country with Merle, he'd be next to impossible to track."

"And once we headed back to Tennessee, he'd bring Merle back to Israel," Mrs. Gomez continued.

"If it weren't for Merle's brilliant

clue-leaving skills!" Justin said enthusi-
astically.

"Well, *brilliant* might not be the best
word, dear," Pearl said, knowing her
husband better. "He usually doesn't
think that far ahead. I'd go with
fortunate. And maybe change *skills*
to *accidents*."

"If it weren't for Merle's fortunate clue-leaving accidents!" Justin revised.

"Much better," Pearl concluded.

"Whether on purpose or by accident, it's the only clue we have," Michael said. "But how do we cross the Jordan and track Merle in a van towing a donkey trailer?"

"We can't cross here," Dr. Gomez replied. "Along with being highly illegal, it's also highly impractical. They are on foot along a riverbed."

"Then that's where we need to be!" Michael said. After a short discussion, the group decided to split up. Dr. Gomez, Michael, Justin, and Dusty would strike out on foot along Israel's west bank of the river. The river is not that wide, so they believed they would be able to spot Ruben on the other side. Mrs. Gomez, Sadie, Pearl, Jane, and Adriana would drive the van to the Allenby Bridge, which crosses the Jordan about ten miles to the north.

"If we don't spot Ruben and Merle before the bridge, we can meet up there and cross into Jordan," Dr. Gomez concluded.

"Girls versus boys!" Sadie said. "Betcha we find 'em first!"

"Yeah, we'll see about that!" Michael countered.

CHAPTER 10

There are no roads leading to the
mouth of the Jordan River. The mouth
of a river, by the way, is the end
that empties out into a larger body
of water—in this case, the Dead Sea.
In order to reach the mouth of the
Jordan from Kalia Beach without a
rowboat, you need to walk. Thankfully, the terrain is flat and dry, so
it does not take much longer to get
there on land than it does by water.
Also thankfully, the cool winter temperatures are much more conducive
for not dying along the way. Dr.
Gomez, Michael, and Justin packed
enough food and water for a couple

of days atop Dusty's back and headed
out.

"We're gonna find him, right, Dad?"
Michael asked. "Doesn't God want us
to find him?"

"You know, buddy, I'm not sure we can know exactly what God wants in this circumstance," Dr. Gomez answered. "Just that we trust and obey him in everything we do. We may not know where this adventure will lead us, but we can know that he wants what is best for us, and for Merle."

"Hmm." Michael pondered for a moment. "I hope we're not too far behind them," he worried as they walked briskly along the barren shoreline. In reality, they were not too far behind at all and arrived at the mouth of the river just a couple of hours after Ruben and Merle had.

"Look!" Justin shouted as they approached the Jordan's delta, pointing to the other side. (The delta of a river, by the way, is where sand, clay, and gravel carried by the water settles at the river's mouth.) An abandoned rowboat sat alone on the Jordanian beach.

"That's got to be Ruben's boat. Keep your eyes peeled," Dr. Gomez said as the boys turned north to follow the river along its west bank. "It's getting late. We'll have to make camp in a couple of hours."

Meanwhile, Mrs. Gomez, Sadie, Pearl, Jane, and Adriana had sped north along Highway 90, also on the look-out for Ruben and Merle. When they arrived, they parked near the end of the bridge and took turns watching for any sign of the squirrelnapper and his precious cargo.

CHAPTER 11

"I love it when you carry me places!"
Merle sighed casually from the com-
fort of Ruben's backpack, munching
on Ruben's trail mix as they trudged
along the muddy banks of the Jordan
River.

"I love it when you make believe
you're not a talking squirrel," Ruben
replied sarcastically.

"You'd prefer if I kept quiet?"
Merle teased.

"You're a genius," Ruben grunted as he tugged his foot out of a muddy hole. Since ditching the rowboat on the Jordanian shore of the Dead Sea in the late morning, the two had journeyed about five miles north along the east bank of the river. If you're walking on a smooth and even path on a nice day, walking five miles will take you less than two hours. With the rough terrain and the weight of an out-of-shape squirrel on his shoulders, Ruben had been slogging along most of the day. "I feel like we should have seen a church by now."

"Too bad we don't have a map," Merle quipped.

"Hrrrg . . ." Ruben grumbled.

"Is it getting late? I feel like it's get-ting late." Merle yawned. Although he could not see anything outside the pack, it was in fact late afternoon and the sun was sinking low on the horizon. The two would soon need to set up camp.

"I think I've found our home for the night." Ruben sighed grumpily.

"Great!" Merle answered. "An inn? An oasis?"

"A cave," Ruben replied flatly as he headed toward the cliffsides a bit inland.

"A what?!" Merle startled in panic. "Please don't make me sleep in another cave! What if I don't wake up again for another 2,000 years!?" Merle was understandably reluctant to ever step paw in a cave again. But despite his pleas, it was the only shelter available, and Ruben had little other choice.

"I know better than to go into a cave without an experienced guide," Ruben remarked while he set up camp just inside the cave's mouth.

"You gonna let me out of this backpack?" Merle wondered as Ruben settled into a gravelly spot to sleep. Moments later, Merle's question was answered by the ring of a heavy snore. "I suppose not," he concluded.

CHAPTER 12

Merle groaned groggily from the darkness of the zipped-up backpack, waking from a deep sleep.

SCRATCH! SCRATCH! SCRATCH!

"All right, I'm up already," Merle complained. Expecting to hear Ruben's voice in reply, he only heard his captor snoring lightly across the cave. "Who's there?" Merle asked after a moment, knowing it must be someone or something other than Ruben.

He was greeted with the exact same question. "Who's there?" the surprised voice asked.

Is my voice echoing? Merle wondered. "I asked first," he whispered.

The voice also whispered in response. "What are you doing in there?"

"Before I answer your questions, let me remind you that I asked first," Merle said.

"Oh, fine! My name is Dave," the voice answered.

"Okay, Dave. I'm Merle," Merle replied. "My turn again. What do you want?"

Merle heard a skittering, snuffling sound. Then Dave said, "I smell food."

Uh-oh, Merle thought. Was *he* the food? "Umm . . . what kind of food are we talking about here?"

"Honey," Dave said. "I smell honey. I love honey."

This didn't make Merle feel too much better, knowing that bears love honey. And possibly also love squirrels. Ruben's snores continued to fill the cave. *This may be my only chance for escape*, Merle thought. "Tell you what," Merle finally offered. "If you get me out of here, you can have the honey—if you promise not to eat me."

"Are you a locust?" Dave asked.

"What?! No," Merle replied, stunned by the question. The idea of a talking insect seemed ridiculous to the talking squirrel.

"Then I promise not to eat you," Dave continued.

"Deal," Merle agreed. With Merle pushing on the back of the zipper from the inside and Dave pulling on the head of the zipper from the outside, the two managed to unzip the backpack. As the morning light streamed through the opening in the pack, Merle was greeted by the sight of a bright-blue . . .

. . . lizard.

CHAPTER 13

"Oh good, you're not a bear," whispered Merle, careful not to wake Ruben, who slept facing the cave wall. "Are you a Lizard of Judah, by any chance?" He slipped out of the backpack, one arm curled around the neck of Ruben's honey bear, the other clutching the near-empty bag of trail mix.

Dave lifted his head proudly in the morning sun, letting the rays catch his blue highlights. "Sinai agama is my technical name," he said. "But the ones of us who can talk do go by Lizard of Judah, yes. Why do you ask?"

"Because someone I know was looking for you," Merle said. "Or one like you." He tiptoed toward the cave entrance, lugging the honey behind him.

Dave followed quietly behind. "Who's looking?"

"Shhhhh!" Merle gestured at Ruben. "Don't wake this guy or we'll both end up in his petting zoo."

"Mmmmrghhh," Ruben mumbled sleepily as he rolled over toward the escaping squirrel and lizard, his eyes half-open. Merle and Dave froze in place, terrified. After a moment, however, they realized that even though his eyes were open, Ruben was still sleeping.

"That's creepy," Merle whispered as the two continued their stealthy sneak out of the cave.

Once outside and safely beyond the earshot of Ruben, Merle explained, "The people who captured me would also want to capture you. They're building a talking-animal theme park—and there's a cage with your name on it."

"Hold that thought," Dave said abruptly and flashed past Merle toward an unsuspecting locust resting on a nearby rock.

CRUNCH!

Dave snagged the bug in his mouth.
Then, transferring the insect to one
claw, he reached out with the other.
"Would you mind?"

"Oh. Right," Merle said and handed
Dave the honey. Dave squeezed a glob
of the sweet treat onto the poor crea-
ture, then stuck the whole thing in his
mouth with another *CRUNCH*. The lizard's eyes rolled back as he savored the
taste.

"Mmmm. Mmmm. Mmmm," Dave
murmured in ecstasy as he munched
away while Merle looked on in horror.
"I'm sorry. That was rude," Dave

apologized with a full mouth. He then zipped past Merle and grabbed another locust. "Would you like one? Locusts and honey! My favorite—so delicious! The breakfast of champions!"

"Um. No . . . Thank you, I'm . . . I'm good," Merle stuttered.

"Suit yourself," Dave replied with a shrug before dousing the second insect in honey and gulping it down.

"Thank you very much for getting me out of that backpack," Merle said over Dave's munching.

"Thank YOU. It's been ages since I've had any honey," Dave said after a gulp.

"I'm wondering," Merle continued as Dave licked his claws, "if I might ask for one other favor?"

CHAPTER 14

A short time later, Ruben opened his eyes from his gravelly bed with a yawn. He stood, dusted himself off, and went to gather some dry brush from the surrounding hillside. Piling up his assortment of twigs and sticks, he pulled a match from his pocket and lit the wood.

"Time to get up, Merle," Ruben announced as he set a tin of water over the fire to heat for his morning tea.

If you've been camping before, you know it's always a good idea to boil river water before you drink it. This will kill any parasites in the water that can make you sick. So Ruben let his water boil for several minutes before he finally went to his backpack to unzip it.

"We've got a long day of walking ahead of us, Merle."

Ruben's comment was met with silence.

"I need my tea and honey from the pack," he stated.

Nothing.

"All right, I'm coming in after it," Ruben announced, grabbing the backpack. Right away, he noticed two things: it was much lighter than he remembered AND it was already unzipped!

"MERLE!!!" Ruben yelled, furious. Realizing his morning tea was not going to happen, Ruben quickly gathered his things, snuffed out the campfire, and ran out of the cave, following a set of paw and claw prints toward the river, in search of his runaway squirrel.

CHAPTER 15

Can you guess the other favor Merle
asked Dave for?

"You want me to help you across
the river?" Dave clarified as the two
scurried down from the cliffsides
toward the Jordan. "Don't you know
how to swim?" The truth is, while
squirrels are not the greatest of swimmers, most can squirrel paddle in a
pinch. Merle, however, was not one
of those squirrels.

"I never learned how," Merle admit-
ted with a touch of embarrassment.
In his defense, he did grow up in
Nazareth, which is far removed from
any large body of water. Pearl, on the

other hand, grew up along the Sea of Galilee and was a great swimmer.

"For most of us," Dave added, referring to animals in general, "it's not about learning. We just kind of do it naturally."

"All right, I admit it. I'm scared," Merle confessed.

"Scared of what?" Dave asked.

"Of sinking! What else?" Merle replied.

"But you're so fluffy. There's no way something so fluffy can sink," Dave theorized.

A big reason Merle had wanted to visit the Dead Sea back in the day was that he had heard the salt content made it impossible to sink. He had found this to be true. However, he knew the Jordan River water was salt-free. "I don't want to take any chances," Merle said.

"By the way, what was that about a petting zoo?" Dave asked.

73

Merle explained Dr. Simon's nefarious plan to collect talking animals from all over Israel, including him and Pearl and a Lizard of Judah.

"Well, I'm not the only one," Dave commented, "but none of us would like being stuck in a petting zoo. . . . Not that a scratch behind the ears now and then would be so terrible."

As they approached the riverbank, Merle noticed a number of wooden-roofed structures scattered about and a large, beautiful domed church. A number of tourists were milling around, so Merle and Dave were careful not to attract attention and ducked behind a big stone near the river.

"What is this place?" Merle whispered.

"Bethany Beyond the Jordan," Dave

explained. "The place where Jesus was baptized by his cousin John. John the Baptist! Who, for your information, also appreciated the local cuisine!" Dave snagged another locust, doused it with honey, and crunched it down.

"I just spent the last few months in a birdcage in Ein Karem, where John was born," Merle told Dave, who raised a brow. "Long story. . . . Why did John baptize Jesus?"

CHAPTER 16

SQUIRREL'S-EYE **VIEW**

Dave had heard the story from the Bethany Beyond the Jordan tour guides many times. "When Jesus was about thirty years old, he traveled here from his home in Nazareth."

"That's where I'm from too!" Merle said.

"Then you know it was a long walk!" Dave added. "Most people at the time came here to be baptized by John the Baptist, to repent of the wrong things they had done. John would tell them, "Repent of your sins and turn to God, for the Kingdom of Heaven is near!"

"What about Jesus?" Merle asked.

"He came here to be baptized too."

"But Jesus never sinned!" Merle protested. "Why would he need to be baptized?"

"John had that question too." Dave nodded. "When John saw Jesus arrive here at the river, he tried to stop him. John said, 'Jesus, I need to be baptized by you, not the other way around.' But Jesus was baptized anyway, to show his choice to follow God's will by saving everyone from the wrong things they had done."

"John's parents, Elizabeth and Zechariah, must have told John about the miraculous birth of Jesus?" Merle guessed. Merle remembered the story Dusty had told him in Ein Karem about Mary, pregnant with Jesus, visiting Elizabeth, and how

John leaped for joy in Elizabeth's tummy.

"Of course," Dave answered. "John knew Jesus was special, but he had no idea how special he was until after he baptized him."

"Why?" Merle wondered. "What happened then?"

"When Jesus came up out of the water, the sky above opened up!" Dave said, motioning dramatically with his front claws to the clouds above before linking them together in a bird shape. "John saw the Spirit of God coming down and resting on Jesus like a dove," Dave stated and rested his bird/claws on Merle's head for a moment before continuing. "John then heard a voice from heaven saying, "This is my much-loved Son. I am very happy with him."

"Whoa," Merle marveled.

"Yeah," Dave agreed. "John realized at that moment that Jesus was the King he had been telling everyone about!"

CHAPTER 17

"Have you seen a squirrel running around?" Ruben's voice rang out across the historic site. Merle and Dave poked their heads out from behind their boulder on the riverside.

"Oh no!" Merle whispered, spotting Ruben in the distance speaking with a couple of tourists.

"Can squirrels even live around here?" one of the confused tourists asked.

Merle and Dave ducked back behind the rock.

"I've got to get across the river!" Merle pleaded. "Help me!"

"Look," Dave replied nervously, "I'll

level with you. I'm not afraid of swim-
ming, but I am afraid of being eaten.
You're big enough to not be swallowed
by a catfish, but I'm not." The lizard's fears were well-founded; catfish
in the Jordan are big and hungry
and wouldn't be likely to pass up the
sight of a small reptile wiggling in the
water over their heads. "I lost a cousin
that way!"

"It's not just me. We BOTH have to
get out of here," Merle argued, "before
Ruben slaps the two of us in his backpack!" Merle looked around nervously.
Was there another way to cross? He
saw no bridge or trees with branches
that he could jump between. But he
did see something that gave him an
idea.

"Hold on a second," Merle whispered.

He crept out from behind the boulder, careful not to be seen by Ruben, and snagged a crumpled map that lay discarded on the ground. Merle retreated back behind the stone. "What would you think about boating across?" he said as he began to fold.

Moments later, Merle had constructed a small origami boat.

"How are we gonna fit in there?"
Dave wondered.

"I'm not," Merle said as he grabbed
a large palm frond and rested it
between the top of the boulder and the
edge of the water like a ramp. "You're
gonna ride the boat so you don't get
eaten, and pull me behind so I don't
have to swim." Merle picked up a
couple of sticks and tested one against
his hind paw.

Have you ever seen a picture or a movie of a squirrel water-skiing? (It's one of the biggest things on the internet.) If you have, you'll be able to picture what it looked like for Dave in an origami boat to zip down a palm frond ramp pulling Merle, standing on two sticks like water skis.

"Wheeeeeee!" they both shouted, with paws and claws in the air, launching across the surface of the Jordan.

Ruben turned toward the sound. "Get back here!!!" he yelled as he sprinted toward the waterfront. He dove headfirst with outstretched hands toward the water-skiing squirrel, missing Merle by mere inches before splashing down into the river. The swell created by Ruben's body propelled the escapees even faster as they rode the wave across to the opposite bank, Dave steering the paper boat with his tail.

"Sir!" a guard yelled at Ruben as his head popped back up above water. "Baptisms do not start until nine!"

CHAPTER 18

"WOO-HOO! We made it!" Merle cele-
brated as he and Dave climbed out of
the water on the western riverbank. He
gave Dave a high four. (Just in case
you're wondering, squirrels have four
toes on their front paws and five on
their back.) Merle and Dave looked
back across the river to see Ruben
being pulled out by the guard.

"I've never been on this side of the
river," Dave commented. "Where to
now?"

"Hmm . . ." Merle pondered, looking
around. He glanced south along the
river toward the Dead Sea. There was
no way he was going back there. West

led to Jerusalem beyond the Judean Desert. However, he had crossed that desert once before with Ruben, Pearl, and Dusty, loaded with a whole donkey pack of supplies. Even with the cooler winter temperatures, he'd never make it on foot without water. Finally, he looked north toward Galilee. "North," Merle finally replied. "If we keep along the river, it'll lead to the Sea of Galilee."

"Sounds like a plan," Dave said. "What's the Sea of Galilee?"

"It's a giant lake. My wife, Pearl, and I began a raft ride down the Jordan from there once. Maybe if I can make it back to that spot where we started our trip, Pearl will figure out where to find me."

"Aww, that's sweet," Dave replied.

"You're a sentimental squirrel, aren't you, Merle?"

"I guess I am," Merle noted. "Would you like to join me? I could use the company!"

"Sure," Dave replied, happy to continue hanging out with his new friend. "Actually, it's probably good for me to lie low, as long as this Dr. Simon guy is looking for me. And I can eventually find a spot to cross over the river and head back home."

"Sounds like a plan!" Merle said.

CHAPTER 19

"Welcome to Qasr al-Yahud," Dr. Gomez said as he, Michael, Justin, and Dusty approached a tower beside a church surrounded by palm trees and tall grasses. An amphitheater built into the bank of the river was filled with a crowd, mostly dressed in white robes, witnessing a baptism.

Had they arrived just thirty minutes earlier, the group would have clearly seen Merle and Dave riding across the river on their Ruben wave. But unfortunately, they got a late start that morning when Dusty wandered too close to the river while eating reeds for breakfast and got stuck in the mud.

"In Arabic, the name means 'the Tower of the Jews,'" Dusty said in full tour-guide mode as the mud-caked group paused to take in the view. As a Holy Land donkey, Dusty had been to the site many times and knew the program. "According to tradition, this is the spot where Joshua and the Israelites crossed over the Jordan and into the Holy Land. It's also where

Elijah crossed in the opposite direction before being taken up into heaven in a chariot of fire."

"Well done, Dusty!" complimented Dr. Gomez. "Do you guest lecture?"

"Cool," Justin said, looking to the eastern sky and imagining flaming chariots.

Michael scanned the near and far banks of the river, looking for any sign of Ruben or Merle, but all he saw was the crowds. "Why are people getting baptized?" Michael wondered.

"This site also commemorates the baptism of Jesus," Dr. Gomez said. "Many people travel here and to Bethany Beyond the Jordan, on the other side of the river in the country of Jordan, to be baptized."

"Why are there two locations?"

Justin asked. "Where was Jesus *really* baptized?"

"Over the centuries, the course of the Jordan has shifted slightly," Dr. Gomez continued. "It happens to all rivers; they're not like mountains or seas, which tend to stay put. So it's not fully clear which is closest to the real location—but most experts think it was the Jordan site."

"Makes sense." Michael nodded and took out Merle's origami map. "How far to the bridge now?"

"About ten kilometers—or six miles—walking," Dusty said.

"Then let's keep going," Dr. Gomez said. "Mom will be waiting." The boys continued north, keeping their eyes out for Merle and Ruben on the opposite bank of the river.

CHAPTER 20

"That's him!" Sadie shouted from
the front passenger seat of the van.
The girls had camped out in the van
near the Allenby Bridge and now had
a pair of binoculars trained on the
checkpoint.

"Merle?!" Pearl squeaked as she hopped up on Sadie's shoulder.

"No, the man in the suit and sunglasses!" Sadie clarified, pointing to Ruben as he passed through the bridge's pedestrian checkpoint from Jordan to Israel. His suit and hair were caked in dried mud, and among the other crisp and freshly showered border crossers, he stuck out like a sore thumb.

What is Ruben doing at the bridge, you ask?! A couple of hours earlier, after his failed attempt to re-nab Merle, the soggy and exhausted squirrel-napper hurried north to the bridge in an attempt to head off Merle and Dave. Since the river is a heavily guarded international border for humans, attempting to swim across was not an option for him. Ruben's only alternative to get back into Israel was to cross at the bridge.

"What do we do?!" Sadie wondered.

"I've got an idea!" Pearl said, rubbing her paws together.

"Oh, hi, Ruben!" Pearl chirped tauntingly moments later from beside their empty church van outside the border control station. "What in the world are you doing here?" The sliding side door sat wide open behind her.

"Huh? Wha . . . Whe . . . ?" Ruben fumbled for words. He'd been so laser-focused on recapturing Merle the whole morning—and on hunting down an elusive Lizard of Judah—that the sight of Pearl, whom he had last seen in Bethlehem successfully escaping atop an alpaca, had him tongue-tied.

"You don't happen to know where Merle is, do you?" Pearl continued as she hopped up into the van and onto an armrest. "I sure would love to find him." She smiled.

The sight of Pearl cornered in a vehicle was too tempting for Ruben to pass up. What luck! She'd be the perfect replacement for the lost Merle!

As Ruben lunged toward Pearl, she bounded to the driver's seat. Sadie pulled the driver's door open just wide enough for Pearl to squeeze out, then closed the door again. Ruben, now sensing a trap, turned around quickly, only to be met with the backside of Adriana the alpaca, her head turned toward him.

"Hmm . . ." Adriana hummed before giving Ruben a powerful and swift kick to the stomach with her hind legs.

Ruben grunted as he flew backward, limbs sprawling, into the van and onto the center bench seat. Immediately, Jane slid the side door shut and Mrs. Gomez locked the child safety–enabled doors with a click of the remote.

"Gotcha!" Pearl shouted.

CHAPTER 21

If capturing Ruben were not exciting enough, two other dramatic events occurred just moments after that. The first was that Dr. Gomez, Michael, Justin, and Dusty, hearing the familiar voices of the girls and commotion in the distance, sprinted up from the riverbed to find Ruben pounding on the van windows.

"Let me out of here!" Ruben shouted, his voice muffled by the glass.

"Not until you give us back Merle!" Pearl replied.

"Wow, nice job!" Michael marveled. "How'd you manage to catch him?"

Sadie smiled and high-fived Pearl, Jane, and Mrs. Gomez. "Just a little teamwork," she said.

"Hmm . . ." Adriana added.

"Ruben—what did you do with Merle?" Dr. Gomez demanded through the glass.

The disheveled squirrelnapper crossed his arms defiantly. "I don't have him. He escaped this morning."

Pearl smiled. While she was disappointed that Ruben was not in possession of her husband, she couldn't help but be proud knowing that he had bested their squirrelnapper. "Way to go, Merle!" she whispered.

"So what do we do with him now?" Justin wondered.

"Why is everyone so muddy?" Jane asked.

Are you wondering what the other dramatic event was? A few hundred yards away, down by the riverside and out of earshot from the hubbub above them, a squirrel and a lizard passed beneath the Allenby Bridge.

"You might be able to cross over here," Merle suggested to Dave, knowing that the lizard eventually needed to get back home.

"Nah. Too many people up there," Dave replied. "A blue lizard on a white bridge is too easy to spot. I'd end up in that zoo you keep telling me about. Or as some kid's pet."

"Eh, that might not be so bad," Merle noted, thinking of his spacious hamster home in Michael's bedroom back in Tennessee.

"Besides, I'm enjoying our walk,"

Dave said. "How long until we reach the Sea of Galilee?"

"Your guess is as good as mine." Merle shrugged as the two new buddies continued north.

"I'm a happy lizard, walking in the sun," Dave sang.

"You're a happy lizard . . . I hope you're having fun," Merle added in song.

"That's not how it goes," Dave corrected.

Tel Aviv
"The only zoo where cuddly creatures talk to you."
Woo-hoo! Hayride!
ALLENBY BRIDGE
Where John baptized Jesus!
Bethany Beyond the Jordan
Kalia Beach
Jerusalem
Bethlehem
Not here again!
Dead Sea
AHHH! Peeping donkey!
Excuse me, miss!
TOUR GUIDE

MICHAEL GOMEZ is an adventurous and active 10-year-old boy. He is kindhearted but often acts before he thinks. He's friendly and talkative and blissfully unaware that most of his classmates think he's a bit geeky. Michael is super excited to be in fifth grade, which, in his mind, makes him "grade school royalty!"

MERLE SQUIRREL may be thousands of years old, but he never really grew up. He has endless enthusiasm for anything new and interesting—especially this strange modern world he finds himself in. He marvels at the self-refilling bowl of fresh drinking water (otherwise known as a toilet) and supplements his regular diet of tree nuts with what he believes might be the world's most perfect food: chicken nuggets. He's old enough to know better, but he often finds it hard to do better. Good thing he's got his wife, Pearl, to help him make wise choices.

PEARL SQUIRREL is wise beyond her many, many, many years, with enough common sense for both her and Merle. When Michael's in a bind, she loves to share a lesson or bit of wisdom from Bible events she witnessed in her youth. Pearl's biggest quirk is that she is a nut hoarder. Having come from a world where food is scarce, her instinct is to grab whatever she can. The abundance and variety of nuts in present-day Tennessee can lead to distraction and storage issues.

111

JUSTIN KESSLER is Michael's best friend.
Justin is quieter and has better judgment than
Michael, and he is super smart. He's a rule
follower and is obsessed with being on time.
He'll usually give in to what Michael wants
to do after warning him of the likely conse-
quences.

SADIE HENDERSON is Michael and Justin's other best friend. She enjoys video games and bowling just as much as cheerleading and pajama parties. She gets mad respect from her classmates as the only kid at Walnut Creek Elementary who's not afraid of school bully Edgar. Though Sadie's in a different homeroom than her two best friends, the three always sit together at lunch and hang out after class.

DR. GOMEZ, a professor of anthropology, is not thrilled when he finds out that his son, Michael, smuggled two ancient squirrels home from their summer trip to the Dead Sea, but he ends up seeing great value in having them around as original sources for his research. Dad loves his son's adventurous spirit but wishes Michael would look (or at least peek) before he leaps.

MRS. GOMEZ teaches part-time at her daughter's preschool and is a full-time mom to Michael and Jane. She feels sorry for the fish-out-of-water squirrels and looks for ways to help them feel at home, including constructing and decorating an over-the-top hamster mansion for Merle and Pearl in Michael's room. She also can't help but call Michael by her favorite (and his least favorite) nickname, Cookies.

MR. NEMESIS is the Gomez family cat who becomes Merle and Pearl's true nemesis. Jealous of the time and attention given to the squirrels by his family, Mr. Nemesis is continuously coming up with brilliant and creative ways to get rid of them. He hides his ability to talk from the family, but not the squirrels.

JANE GOMEZ is Michael's little sister. She's super adorable but delights in getting her brother busted so she can be known as the "good child." She thinks Merle and Pearl are the cutest things she has ever seen in her whole life (next to Mr. Nemesis) and is fond of dressing them up in her doll clothes.

RUBEN, previously known only as "the man in the suit and sunglasses," has been on the squirrels' tails ever since Michael discovered them at the Dead Sea. Ruben is determined to capture and deliver the refugee rodents to his boss in Israel. He's clever and inventive, but then again, so are the squirrels! Ruben struggles to stay one step ahead of Merle and Pearl.

DR. SIMON is the director of the Jerusalem Antiquities Museum and Ruben's boss. The mastermind behind the creation of the world's first and largest talking-animal petting zoo, he'll stop at nothing to make sure Merle and Pearl headline the grand opening of his theme park alongside a bevy of other babbling biblical beasts.

FATHER PHILLIP is a kind and helpful friar who first encounters Merle and Pearl at the Basilica of the Annunciation in Nazareth. He becomes a trusted local ally of Dr. Gomez and Michael, keeping an ear to the ground for the whereabouts of the squirrels as they are smuggled about Israel.

ADRIANA hails from South America (like all alpacas), so how did she end up in Israel? No one knows for sure, but what is certain is that Adriana is the best friend a donkey could ask for and president of the Dusty Fan Club. She can't speak, but she can pick locks with her lips and has a knack for being in the right place at the right time.

DUSTY is a retired Holy Land tour donkey, purchased by Ruben for agorot on the shekel (pennies on the dollar) to transport Merle and Pearl from Galilee to Judea. The squirrels soon discover that Dusty can also speak human and is a direct descendant of Balaam's donkey of biblical fame.

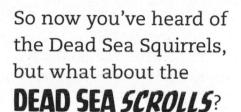

DR. GOMEZ'S
Historical Handbook

So now you've heard of the Dead Sea Squirrels, but what about the **DEAD SEA *SCROLLS*?**

Way back in 1946, just after the end of World War II, in a cave along the banks of the Dead Sea, a 15-year-old boy came across some jars containing ancient scrolls while looking after his goats. When scholars and archaeologists found out about his discovery, the hunt for more scrolls was on! Over the next 10 years, many more scrolls and pieces of scrolls were found in 11 different caves.

There are different theories about exactly who wrote on the scrolls and hid them in the caves. One of the most popular ideas is that they belonged to a group of Jewish priests called Essenes, who lived in the desert because they had been thrown out of Jerusalem. One thing is for sure—the scrolls are very, very old! They were placed in the caves between the years 300 BC and AD 100!

Forty percent of the words on the scrolls come from the Bible. Parts of every Old Testament book except for the book of Esther have been discovered.

Of the remaining 60 percent, half are religious texts not found in the Bible, and half are historical records about the way people lived 2,000 years ago.

The discovery of the Dead Sea Scrolls is one of the most important archaeological finds in history!

About the Author

As co-creator of VeggieTales, co-founder
of Big Idea Entertainment, and the voice
of the beloved Larry the Cucumber,
MIKE NAWROCKI has been dedicated
to helping parents pass on biblical
values to their kids through storytelling
for over two decades. Mike currently
serves as assistant professor of film and
animation at Lipscomb University in
Nashville, Tennessee, and makes his
home in nearby Franklin with his wife,
Lisa, and their two children. The Dead
Sea Squirrels is Mike's first children's
book series.

A TALKING FISH?

CHAOS IN A FRUIT MARKET?

A SQUIRREL REUNION?!?

Find out what happens
in the next
Dead Sea Squirrels book!

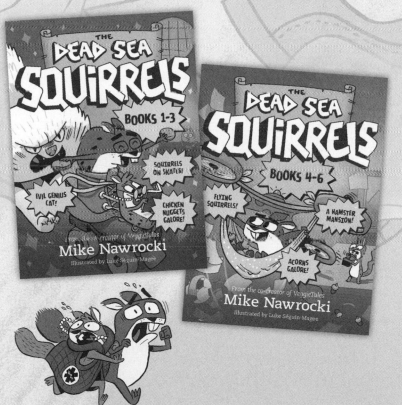

SADDLE UP AND JOIN WINNIE AND HER FAMILY AT THE WILLIS WYOMING RANCH!

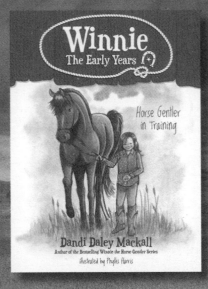

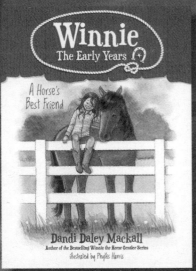

Winnie is the star of the bestselling Winnie the Horse Gentler series that sold more than half a million copies and taught kids around the world about faith, kindness, and horse training. Winnie could ride horses before she could walk, but training them is another story. In this new series, eight-year-old Winnie learns the fine art of horse gentling from her horse wrangler mom as they work together to save the family ranch.